FAST & FURIOUS
SPY RACERS

FROM GEARS
TO GADGETS

A COMPANION GUIDE

BY JORDAN GERSHOWITZ

PENGUIN YOUNG READERS LICENSES
An Imprint of Penguin Random House LLC, New York

Published by Penguin Young Readers Licenses,
an imprint of Penguin Random House LLC, New York. Printed in the USA.

Visit us online at www.penguinrandomhouse.com.

ISBN 9780593096321   10 9 8 7 6 5 4 3 2 1

START YOUR ENGINES!

It's time to gear up for the thrill-seeking, globe-trotting Netflix series *Fast & Furious: Spy Racers*. Inspired by the blockbuster film franchise, *Fast & Furious: Spy Racers* introduces the world to a new generation of heroes—led by the charismatic Tony Toretto.

Now that they've successfully saved the world from the villainous organization known as SH1FT3R, Tony and the Spy Racers are taking their talents to South America to investigate a mysterious criminal element in Rio. When they get there, the Spy Racers discover a plot to put the whole city under mind control and must win a massive race through the winding streets of the Brazilian favelas. Luckily, the Spy Racers are outfitted with the most extreme, tricked-out vehicles and the latest spy technology, which will help them pull off this mission like no other team could.

So buckle up, *Fast & Furious* fans, because as the newest member of Tony's crew, you're in for one pulse-pounding, high-octane ride!

TABLE OF CONTENTS

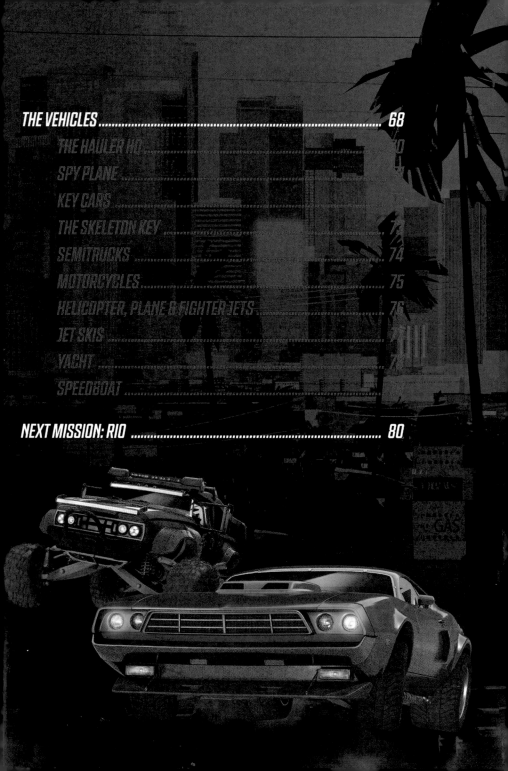

THE HEROES

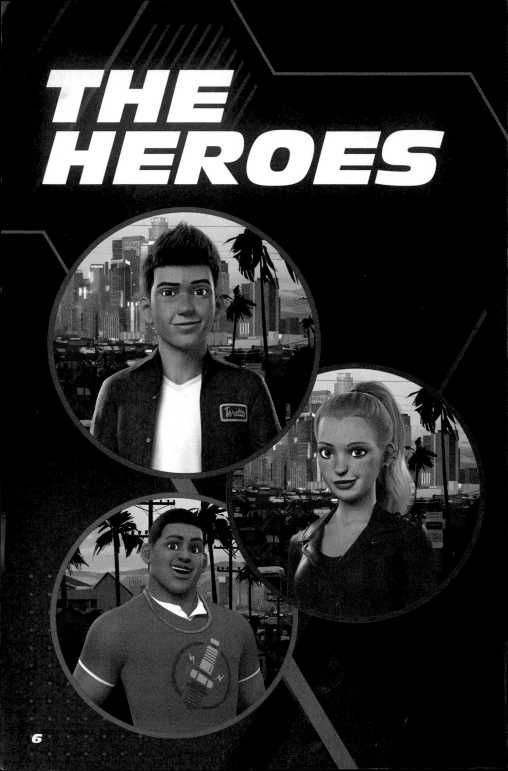

TONY
TORETTO

THE LEADER

A born competitor who hates to lose, Tony is one of the best drivers in Los Angeles. He dreams of being a racing legend like his cousin Dom, the leader of a group of elite racers turned international heroes. Dom is a man with a strong moral code who values his ride-or-die family more than anything else. Tony hopes to live (and race!) just like him.

When Dom recruits Tony and his crew to join Ms. Nowhere's secret government spy organization, Tony is immediately ready for action. This speed addict feels he has a lot to prove, and he'll push himself to the edge to find out what he's really made of.

While Tony's supreme confidence and loyalty occasionally lead him to take some pretty huge risks, he is also smart and knows a good driver is nothing without their crew. Luckily for him, Tony has one of the best crews on earth.

"I'M NOT JUST FOLLOWING ORDERS, I'M FOLLOWING MY GUT."

ION MOTORS THRESHER

Speed Boosters:

Made famous by Tony's cousin Dom, this energy boost gives an increase in horsepower. If anyone even wants to sniff the finish line thanks to a burst of torque and speed, they'd better make sure they're packing one of these in their engine.

Precision Engine:

Hold on tight! When Tony hits a red button on the side of his steering wheel, rocket fuel pumps into his engine . . . giving his car 1,000 horsepower.

Night Vision:

Tony never needs to be afraid of the dark when he's in his whip. All he has to do is flip this switch, and his windshield turns into a video monitor, which thankfully helps him see clearly while driving at night or in tunnels. Bad guys always seem to want to be chased at night!

Spy Defense Systems:

If Tony's in a jam, all he has to do is press a few buttons, and flaps on the side of his car will open, transforming the Ion Thresher into the *ultimate* defense machine. With rockets hidden under the hood, missiles in the grille, and thrusters in the trunk, this car is *not* to be messed with.

Spikes:

These extend from Tony's tires, giving him extra traction for hairpin turns and dangerous terrain, like when he's driving on the side of a cliff!

ADDITIONAL SPY MODIFICATIONS

REAR JETS: ▬

Always handy for when Tony needs a super boost to launch his ride into the air. It can help Tony jump over small cars, big cars, and even a giant canyon!

ROCKETS: ▬

Get ready for blastoff! Activated from the dashboard, these rear rockets allow Tony to drive so fast, it feels like he's flying.

SMOKE SCREEN TIRES: ▬

When Tony does doughnuts with his car, the tires emit an insane amount of smoke that obstructs the view of any vehicle within the vicinity.

PAINTBALL SHOOTERS:

You better grab a smock when Tony starts firing these bad boys! This paintball launcher makes other vehicles look like a Picasso painting.

GRAPPLING HOOK:

If Tony wants to hitch a ride on another car, a semi, or even a helicopter, all he has to do is activate this grappling hook, which grabs ahold of anything it latches onto. Because why wouldn't you want to hitch a ride on a chopper?

GEARS & GADGETS

MAGNET HANDS:

During the Yoka Spirit Water heist, Tony heroically leaps out of his car and uses these to stick to the side of a moving semitruck. Shashi, the leader of SH1FT3R, is so impressed that he welcomes Tony into the criminal organization. Who knew magnet hands could come in . . . *handy*?

EXPLOSIVES:

Fire in the hole! Tony uses these explosives to dislodge the semitruck trailer from its cab during the Yoka Spirit Water heist. A word of advice to Tony for next time (because we all know there will be a next time): Make sure you're off the truck before detonating.

SPY WATCH:

Given to Tony by Ms. Nowhere, this watch allows its user to communicate via hologram. When Tony goes to Rio, his watch is able to remotely start up and pilot his car from a distance.

WINGSUIT:

One might be nervous about jumping out of a spy plane that's ten thousand feet in the air, but not Tony. As long as he has his trusty wingsuit, this hero can leap from the most extreme heights, like even a roller coaster, and always glide to safety. This kid has skills!

SHOCK GLOVES:

Electric-powered gloves that shock whatever they touch. It should be obvious, but WARNING: Do *not* high-five your friends with these!

This seventeen-year-old environmentalist legally changed her name to her street tag, Echo. Her real name is Margaret, but don't ever call her that. You don't want to be on Echo Pearl's bad side!

Echo has never met a wall she hasn't painted or an authority figure she hasn't scorned. As a master artist, she loves upcycling trash into art as much as she loves messing with people's heads. When it comes to wielding a spray paint can or rigging up the coolest underbody light package, there's no one better.

And the only thing Echo loves as much as art? Driving fast. Her self-built electric car goes from zero to sixty in 2.4 seconds. Now that she's a Spy Racer, Echo has discovered she is a natural secret agent as she was integral in saving the world from SH1FT3R.

"I GOTTA **ADMIT,** I LIKE THIS **SPY** STUFF. IT'S AS IF I WAS MADE TO SECRETLY MESS WITH OTHER PEOPLE."

HYPERFIN

Booster Rockets:

No terrain can stop the Spy Racers, not even a giant mountain. When Echo needs more thrust, all she has to do is engage her booster rockets and she'll be flying up the steep Mt. Zebulon in no time.

Subwoofer:

You know it's all about the bass! This subwoofer is a special kind of speaker designed to produce the coolest and loudest thumping bass sounds. DJ air horn sold separately.

Paintball Shooters:

If you thought Echo was skilled with a spray paint can, just wait till you see her use her paintball launcher. When locked onto a target, she'll paint the town . . . and her adversary's car . . . red!

Smoke Bombs:

These weapons can cause some serious car carnage! Like the time the Spy Racers attempted to steal the final Key Car from a military compound. When Echo deployed the smoke bombs, they blinded General Dudley's men, causing them to crash into one another.

Lighting Kit:

Whether it's time to save the day or time to party, these LED interior lights allow Echo to set the mood for any occasion.

ADDITIONAL SPY MODIFICATIONS

SMOKE SCREEN TIRES:

If Echo needs a quick getaway, there's nothing better than these tires. All Echo has to do is peel out and she'll burn so much rubber that her smoke screen will distract anyone on her tail.

OIL MISSILES:

Watch out, slippery road ahead! The cause: Echo, of course! When fired, these oil missiles give enemies a slip-and-slide mess to deal with as they swerve out of control on the track.

EXTENDABLE TIRES:

Echo's tires extend from the body of her car. Sounds techy, but really it just lets her car grip onto walls like a lizard. She can be sideways or upside down and surprise-attack criminals from all sides! It's kind of the coolest.

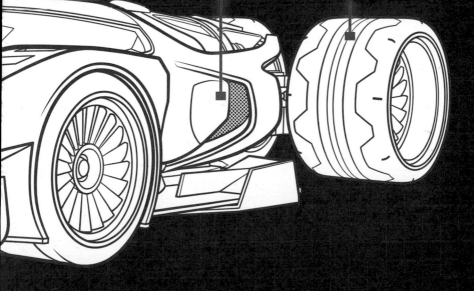

CREEPER:

This modified roller-seat lets Echo attach *and* detach herself to the underside of any car. She most recently used it on the team's mission to destroy the last Key Car.

KNOCKOUT GAS:

What does Echo do when she's surrounded by a team of armed guards in a military hangar? She uses her knockout gas, of course. This weapon is so powerful that anyone who breathes it will instantly fall to the ground, completely unconscious. Sweet dreams, baddies!

SPY BROOCH: ▪

This robotic spider-looking device acts as a tracker and a camera. It is controlled remotely via Echo's phone and has the ability to stream live camera footage to a pair of sunglasses. When incognito, it fastens to Echo's shirt like a pin!

SPY GLASSES: ▪

These glasses are the best gear out there when you need to track down your friends and crew! Echo wears them in Rio to locate a missing Layla. They project a map that shows the lay of the land, and the red blinking dot pinpoints the exact location of Layla's whereabouts. Now all the Spy Racers need is for Layla to stay still . . .

SPY WATCH: ▪

Echo was issued this gadget when she first joined the Spy Racers, but now her watch has the ability to shoot out a grappling hook. This allows her to swing and maneuver from building to building. Pretty cool upgrade, right?

CISCO RENALDO

THE GEARHEAD

Cisco is the muscle of the group. In certain instances, Cisco can display incredible feats of strength, like when he lifted up Tony's crashed car during a SH1FT3R race in an abandoned mine shaft.

But don't let his size fool you; Cisco is also a beast when it comes to ingenuity. His father and uncles taught him how to keep every car up and running using any spare parts they could find, which has made Cisco the greatest junkyard scrounger in the neighborhood. If he can't find what he's looking for, Cisco can weld, grind, and fabricate any part.

Cisco loves being a member of the crew and taking care of everyone. He is as genuine as they come and is especially close with Frostee Benson, who often rides shotgun in Cisco's truck.

"THERE'S NOTHING A LITTLE BUBBLE GUM CAN'T FIX!"

RALLY BAJA CRAWLER

Grappling Hook:

A rope that shoots out of Cisco's car, the grappling hook allows him to tow other vehicles, like the Spy Racers' oversize Hauler.

Rocket Thruster:

Up, up, and away! The Baja Crawler can achieve serious liftoff and climb to the tops of the highest mountains with just the push of a button. Watch out, Mt. Kilimanjaro, Cisco and his thrusters are eyeing you next!

Jack-Up Lever:

When Cisco pulls a lever, his truck "jacks up" and extends, allowing him to clear over other vehicles.

Tech Station:

Everyone calls "shotgun" when they see this passenger seat! A computer lover's dream, Frostee's tech station is equipped with the latest high-def screens, voice-control activations, and advanced graphic chips. Let's be honest, who wouldn't want to play videos games *and* fight bad guys at the same time?

Blind-Spot-Blocking Drones:

They may look small, but these drones sure are important on missions. During the Yoka Spirit Water heist, Frostee and Cisco attach these to Scadan's rearview mirrors, projecting a fake holographic image so the outlaw doesn't know the Spy Racers are actually behind him.

Rocket Engine:

An energy boost that gives this 4×4 more speed! This modification does tend to backfire when most needed—like the time it blew a giant hole in the Baja Crawler's floor, and the Spy Racers got stuck in quicksand. Let that one *sink* in!

GEARS & GADGETS

SPY WATCH:

These watches allow designated users to track the location of other spy watches. They are extremely helpful when a team member gets separated or goes missing . . . which actually happens more than you'd think.

SPY FANNY PACK:

Given to Cisco by Ms. Nowhere when in Rio, this fanny pack holds the team's new spy gear, including Frostee's Nano Drones and Cisco's various spy gums. **BONUS:** It never goes out of style!

LASER CAP:

The Spy Racers don't need a pitching machine when Cisco has a baseball hat that fires laser discs out of its bill. Batter up!

SPY GUM: ■

Different flavors of gum, each with a unique purpose, activated when chewed. A pack of gum that helps save the world *and* cures bad breath? Yes, you read that right. And yes, it's so cool.

Peppermint Gum:
This gum acts as an automotive sealant that is ten times more powerful than the gum currently used to fix cars. Just make sure you don't accidentally glue yourself to the car. That would be embarrassing.

Pink Lemonade Gum:
Like a flashlight on a smartphone, this gum glows brightly when activated to provide visibility.

Green Gum:
This gum forms a molecular bond, like geckos have on their footpads, which allows the user to stick and climb up anything: a wall, a truck, or even a tree while chasing after a monkey!

The Gum That Never Loses Its Flavor:
As implied by the name, this gum can be chewed for twenty-four hours straight and will be just as delicious as when it's first pulled out of its wrapper.

FROSTEE
BENSON

THE HACKER

A thirteen-year-old genius, Frostee tested out of school so he could spend more time with Tony's crew. While he's the only team member who can't drive, everyone in the garage relies on his knowledge, mostly because he's the only one who truly understands the new technology that powers their cars. From remote-controlled racers to drones to a brand-new Italian sports car, Frostee knows how to hack any vehicle's computer and increase its horsepower to monstrous levels. His inventions always come in handy on the team's missions, and he can even remotely pilot a hijacked spy plane with a joystick!

Frostee may be the youngest team member, but he's just as brave as the rest of the crew. When kidnapped by SH1FT3R, Frostee was able to escape *and* discover the Key Cars.

"OOPS, WRONG BUTTON. MOST OF THESE ARE FOR **LASERS,** I GUESS."

GEARS & GADGETS

MEDALLION:

A Swiss Army knife of sorts, this invention is usually found hanging around Frostee's neck. When needed, the medallion can shoot out laser cutters, wirelessly access his computer, and also serve as a lock-picking device.

YOKA HEAD SPY STATION:

Discovered during the Yoka Spirit Water heist, this once promotional beverage display has been retrofitted into a spy station that can track the crew during their missions. Yoka: It refreshes the mind *and* spirit!

PONCHO:

This fiber-optic mesh poncho bends light around its wearer and makes them appear invisible. It's easy to sneak around when no one can see you!

DRONES:

DJ Drone:
This drone not only plays the sickest beats, but it can also blow up cars with its thumping bass. Need a quick getaway or flashing lights for a dance off? Frostee's ultimate party machine can help with both.

Drone Backpack:
When Tony wants to have a street race, Frostee's high-tech backpack releases a drone with built-in speakers and a stoplight, allowing the whiz kid to kick off the race. "Ready, set, GO!"

Large Drone Backpack:
Strap on this backpack and watch it transform into the coolest exo-suit ever. Look out below, because Frostee can now hover and fly like a real superhero!

Ghost Drones:
These devices map out locations, like the abandoned mine shaft, using echolocation. They also have a cloaking device, which can make them appear as ghosts!

VR Headset:
This device gives Frostee a view of the entire racecourse through a drone's POV! The headset also lets Frostee see animated avatars of the racers, including the drivers' stats, their location on the track, and any energy boosts they've used.

Nano Drones:
Housed in Cisco's fanny pack, these drones are controlled remotely by Frostee's modified VR goggles. The drones can set off flashing grenade-like explosions, which cause enemies to become confused and disoriented.

LAYLA GRAY

THE LONE WOLF

Because she's somewhat of a mystery, it's tough to know what side Layla Gray is on. If you ask her, she'd simply answer that she's on "Team Layla."

The loose-cannon daughter of a wealthy Southern family, Layla's rebelled and forged her own sketchy past. She rose through the ranks to become Shashi Dhar's second-in-command and top driver of his criminal racing crew, SH1FT3R.

Layla's wild-card antics have gotten her into trouble all over the world, but she has the grit and racing smarts to back it up. She's whip-smart and bold enough to swagger into any dangerous situation. She loves to drive and hates to admit when she's been bested, especially by Tony. But above everything else, Layla values honesty. When she learns Shashi's true motivations, she flips and helps Tony's crew defeat SH1FT3R. It's this newfound friendship with the Spy Racers that sends the crew to Rio, as Layla has suddenly disappeared while on an undercover mission . . .

"SORRY, ARE YOU TALKING? I'M TOO BUSY WINNING RIGHT NOW."

ASTANA HOTTO

Chain-Driven Circular Saw:

This isn't your grandfather's band saw. With the push of a button, this large weapon extends from Layla's car, and can be used to slice into a foe's vehicle.

Car Magnet:

When SH1FT3R hijacks a high-speed train, Layla and Shashi use their car magnets to lock onto one another and create a makeshift bridge of vehicles. By doing this, SH1FT3R's crew is able to leap onto the moving train.

Grenades:

Cover your eyes! When Layla launches her smoke and flash grenades, it's almost impossible to see, which makes it pretty hard for her opponents to cross the finish line when they don't know where they're going. Just how Layla likes it.

Missiles:

You'd better use caution when tailgating this souped-up ride. If a driver gets too close, Layla will unleash her missiles and take out the competition.

Side Thrusters:

Drivers beware! These thrusters slam vehicles to the edge of the track. Layla even used these to shove Tony toward a wall during their first SH1FT3R race.

MS. NOWHERE

THE HANDLER

A member of a mysterious government agency and an associate of Dom Toretto, Ms. Nowhere is the team's brilliant but prickly secret-agent liaison. Always focused on the mission at hand, Ms. Nowhere often butts heads with the rebellious Tony. Unlike her teenage crew, Ms. Nowhere never makes decisions based on emotion, except for that one time she ate six pints of ice cream because she was in a bad mood. Ms. Nowhere acts like she can't wait to be rid of the team, but she not-so-secretly has a soft spot for them.

As a world-class spy in her own right, Ms. Nowhere enjoys taking down criminals all over the globe and often helps the crew when things get dicey—like the time she plucked a free-falling Tony out of the air with her spy plane.

While Ms. Nowhere is known to have a number of gadgets on her at all times, she also functions as the team's quartermaster, equipping them with all kinds of crazy-cool spy gear and government-grade vehicle upgrades.

"I JUST MADE IT UP TO NOWHERE, AND I WILL NOT GET BUMPED BACK TO MS. NOTHING. I WAS A NOTHING FOR TOO LONG!"

GEARS & GADGETS

TACTICAL PURSE:

This purse not only holds all of Ms. Nowhere's spy equipment, but it also has grappling hooks attached to zip lines that shoot out of each end. Tony and the team "borrow" the purse in order to bust into SH1FT3R's race complex. And the best part? It looks good with any outfit.

PERFUME BOTTLE:

If spritzed, the contents of this bottle act as knockout gas. Just make sure it's pointed in the right direction, or you could end up like Tony and accidentally knock yourself out.

COMPACT MIRROR:

When shaken, this little silver gadget becomes magnetized and activates an EMP (electromagnetic pulse) that is able to shut down the engine of any car.

MAGNETIC HEELS:

While they may look like ordinary shoes, these high heels are equipped with a magnetic grip that allows Ms. Nowhere to cling onto any surface, including the wing of a plane. **DISCLAIMER:** These shoes are *not* sold in stores.

GEARS & GADGETS

JET EXO-SUIT:

Ms. Nowhere loves planes so much, she even has a gadget that turns her into one! This sleek black suit with hard wings and jet engines allows Ms. Nowhere to propel herself through the air like she's a fighter jet.

MILITARY DRONE:

A tactical piece of surveillance equipment, this military drone allows Ms. Nowhere to watch over Tony and the team, especially when they disobey orders.

HIGH-TECH SUNGLASSES:

Perfect for recon missions, these glasses scan for people using facial recognition technology, and they have the ability to zoom in, allowing Ms. Nowhere to survey areas from great distances.

GARY

THE ASSISTANT

As Ms. Nowhere's right hand and lead guard, Gary has a lot of responsibilities: He hands out binders full of information, tracks Tony's crew on their missions, and takes Ms. Nowhere's ire when the team messes up.

Often serving as the comic relief to Ms. Nowhere's cold personality, Gary tries to find the positive in any situation—much to the dismay of his boss. While he may appear nerdy, looks can certainly be deceiving, because Gary is actually an amazing fighter. Thanks to his awesome strength and agility, he can take out a horde of henchmen without breaking a sweat. Gary is also an expert pilot and is tasked with flying the spy plane during some of the most dangerous assignments. Just make sure you don't get captured with Gary, unless you want to hear hours of him playing the harmonica!

"I JUST WANT TO GET SOME COFFEE."

THE VILLAINS

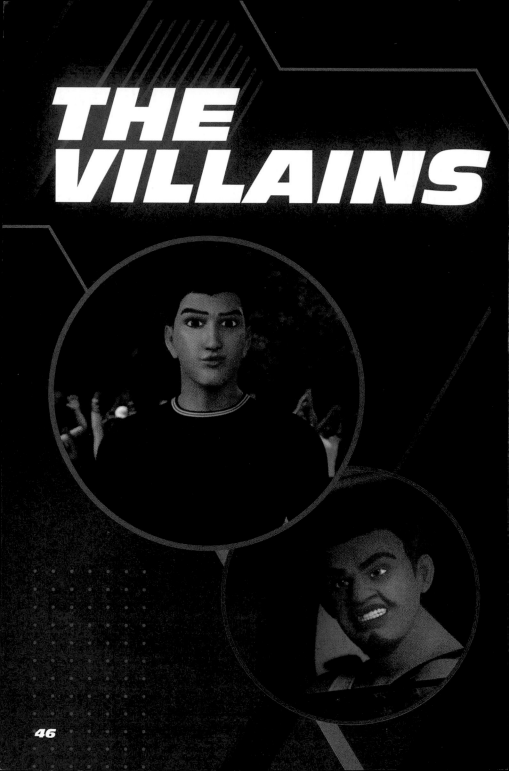

SHASHI
DHAR

THE REVOLUTIONARY

Shashi Dhar is the charismatic leader of the criminal organization SH1FT3R. He's a straight talker who's always in complete control of his emotions. When he gets down to business, though, or if you dare cross him, he can quickly turn from charming to downright frightening because he has a fiery intensity simmering underneath.

With a seemingly unlimited bank account and a treasure trove of tech, Shashi lives his life on the edge and has no respect for authority. He's all about adrenaline, but will break from his lifestyle of illegal racing and extreme sports to steal from some of Silicon Valley's wealthiest people.

However, there is pain in Shashi's past. His parents were genius-level engineers before they were murdered, leaving him an orphan. When Shashi formed SH1FT3R, he hoped to re-create the family he lost, while also using his Robin Hood act as a cover for a diabolical plan to steal the Skeleton Key, a technology that would enable him to take over the world and avenge his parents.

"ONCE YOU MAKE IT INTO SH1FT3R, THE WORLD IS YOURS."

MACALLISTER SUPERFIN

Two-Wheel Drive:

When activated, Shashi's car has the ability to drive on only two wheels, allowing him to squeeze through tight spaces.

Fireworks:

When shot out of Shashi's car, fireworks explode into multicolored smoke that distracts opposing drivers. With this modification, it's Fourth of July every day of the year!

Boosters:

When looking to buy nuclear codes from Sudarikov, a rich Russian weapons dealer, Shashi lets the thug take the Superfin for a joyride. But lending someone your car is not the smartest choice when one of your car's modifications includes an energy boost that gives the car a *massive* speed upgrade.

Grappling Hook:

When Shashi takes the Superfin for a spin with Sudarikov, the Russian accidentally shoots out a grappling hook, which sticks into a nearby cop car. Luckily for these two, they didn't get a ticket!

GEARS & GADGETS

WINGSUIT:

Forget superhero capes, this spy-grade exoskeleton allows Shashi to glide in the air for extended periods of time. Shashi uses this, most notably, when he steals the first Key Car from a billionaire's yacht in the middle of the ocean.

BALLOON GUN:

This gadget fires a large balloon into the air and hooks onto a jet. Shashi uses it to escape tricky situations. Hopefully no one in the SH1FT3R crew is afraid of heights. But if they are . . . better not look down!

VAULT:

Located on a cliff by the water, this palatial mansion houses Shashi's vault, which is full of jewels, priceless artifacts, and, at one point, three Key Cars. Equipped with video cameras, a high-tech security system, and a guard named Rusty, Shashi's mansion is almost impenetrable (if not for the ingenuity of the Spy Racers).

MITCH

THE LOCAL JERK

Hailing from the streets of Los Angeles, Mitch is a trash-talker who seems to only care about two things: one-upping Tony Toretto and eating tacos. Unfortunately for Mitch, he often has trouble doing both of these things.

The quintessential bully, Mitch once beat Tony in a street race thanks to the frankensteined modifications on his car, and he hasn't stopped gloating since. While he may be an adequate racer, Mitch isn't the sharpest tool in the shed, as he's easily outsmarted by the Spy Racers on multiple occasions, like when Echo distracts Mitch so the crew can clone his SH1FT3R crypto-communicator, or later, when they hijack his car to take his spot in a race. While Mitch may be a royal pain for the Spy Racers, he can also be an unlikely ally when the situation calls for it . . . as long as there's something in it for him.

"HEY! MY TACOS ARE IN THERE! MY TACOOO-OOOOS!"

Windbreaker Switch:

Triggered by a button on the dashboard, this modification causes rear thrusters to fire, which allows the car to launch up ramps like a rocket.

The Claw:

A trash-truck-like claw that pops out from under Mitch's car. The claw has a "lift" switch, which extends a hydraulic elbow and can pick opposing cars off the ground.

Grappling Hook:

When Tony uses Mitch's car for his first SH1FT3R race, he fires this gadget into Layla's trunk in an attempt to slow her down. But Tony should have read the directions first, because he accidentally hit the wrong button and pulled himself closer to Layla's weaponized ride.

Rocket Engine:

When engaged, this speed enhancement gives Mitch's car an extra thrust. It is activated by a makeshift handle that Mitch frankensteined onto the dash himself.

CLEVE KELSO

THE EVIL BILLIONAIRE

A billionaire and casino tycoon, Cleve made his bones on the Las Vegas strip when it was run by gangsters. He is now an intimidating force, both in the boardroom and on the streets. A skilled fighter in his own right, Cleve will take matters into his own hands when his underlings can't do the job. As the main investor in the Skeleton Key, Cleve is the focus of Shashi Dhar's fury, because it is revealed that Cleve murdered Shashi's parents when they had finished building him a weapon. While he was able to escape the authorities after the Skeleton Key Battle, something tells the Spy Racers they haven't seen the last of Cleve Kelso.

"YOU SON OF A GUN. I STOLE THAT **MONEY** FAIR AND SQUARE!"

THE SH1FT3R DRIVERS

As the leader of the criminal organization known as SH1FT3R, Shashi Dhar has assembled a tough team of lawbreakers. Each has their own special skills that rival the Spy Racers, including Jun, the London-born hacker, and Nacho and Rollie, the twin terrors who act as Shashi's muscle. Together with the SH1FT3R racers, these delinquents assist in Shashi's quest to gain access to the Skeleton Key and get revenge for his parents' murder.

SCADAN

The Spy Racers first met Scadan, the leader of a rival SH1FT3R crew, when they hijacked his truck full of Yoka Spirit Water—something this tough guy still holds a grudge over. His car has the ability to shoot paintballs, which often causes problems for Tony and the crew.

PIZZARAVE

PizzaRave is a member of SH1FT3R and drives a two-seat roadster with the ability to project weaponized lasers around the car. When locked onto a target, PizzaRave's lasers can explode various objects. PizzaRave's car can also produce a dazzling light show that blinds her opponents. Trust me, this is one rave you *don't* want to be invited to!

SANTIAGO

A member of SH1FT3R, Santiago is known as the greatest driver in South America. However, he wasn't too lucky in his lone race against Tony when he flew off the cliff during Dead Man's Turn. Luckily for Santiago, his car was packed with a parachute, and he was able to float to safety.

TOUGE-DORI

Touge-Dori won her first street race at age thirteen, but was ultimately disqualified because she wasn't even old enough to drive! Since then, she's been tearing up the track as a member of the Japanese drifting team and becoming one of the most skilled racers on the road. The Spy Racers first meet Touge-Dori at a SH1FT3R race in an abandoned mine. Her specialized tuner takes hairpin turns like no one else's, and she's great at knocking other cars off the road.

THE WOOFER

The Woofer's car is loaded with speakers. It has two massive weaponized woofers on the back that can blast music so loudly, they can blow other cars off the track. The vehicle also has an oil-spray attack, which makes the road slippery for those who are unfortunate enough to be driving behind it.

BONEGRINDER

The Spy Racers know they're in trouble when they hear Bonegrinder yell, "First I blind 'em, then I grind 'em!" This mad man drives an oversize monster truck, which can run over and crush anything that gets in its way. Its large frame allows Bonegrinder to handle rugged terrain better than any other SH1FT3R vehicle. And if that's not intimidating enough, his monster truck also has a paintball cannon, which fires projectiles from its chassis.

THE VEHICLES

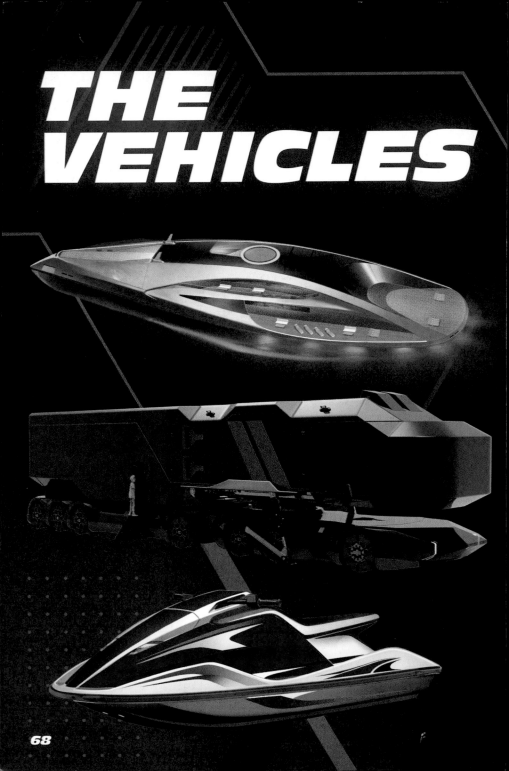

While the Spy Racers use their garage as a home base when in Los Angeles, the Hauler serves as their headquarters for all missions abroad. Issued to the crew by Ms. Nowhere, this vehicle is technologically advanced, with fog-blowing wind jets that extend from the roof, the ability to self-drive, an awesome testing area for the team to run diagnostics on their vehicles, and don't forget about the Froyo machine—Cisco certainly hasn't!

The Hauler also comes equipped with a display table, allowing the Spy Racers to see holographic images of their intended targets and the layout of their upcoming operations. Thanks to Gary, the Hauler will be getting some serious upgrades when the team heads to Rio. And it's a good thing, too, because the Spy Racers will need the Hauler's new transforming wheels to get out of some pretty sticky situations—like quicksand, for starters. It also doesn't hurt to have reinforced armor plating that's so strong, even a cannon blast won't damage this tank!

SPY PLANE

Big enough to fit the massive Hauler inside, this mega spy plane is so large, it can crush a military truck with just one wheel! It serves as the crew's main means of long-distance travel and also acts as a mission control center. While Gary often pilots the plane, it can also be controlled remotely with a joystick. Features include an LED cloaking system that allows the crew to travel undetected, wind jets that extend from the roof, and a kitchen that seems to always be stocked with freshly baked cookies—as long as Cisco saves some for the rest of the crew!

KEY CARS

Made out of an experimental alloy with magnetic signatures, the Key Cars are five separate vehicles that, when brought together to an undisclosed location in the desert, unlock a secret underground facility. This facility houses the Skeleton Key, a device that can take over and control all computerized technology within a several-mile radius. Finding and obtaining all five Key Cars is SH1FT3R's main goal, as Shashi wants to unlock the Skeleton Key to destroy the world order and get revenge on Cleve Kelso, the billionaire who murdered his parents.

THE
SKELETON KEY

An extremely powerful piece of technology, the Skeleton Key is a headset that resembles a skull. The Skeleton Key's vision allows the user to see a grid of the area and control anything computerized within a several-mile radius. Although Ms. Nowhere originally thought the Skeleton Key was a myth, the Spy Racers discover Shashi Dhar's parents created it thanks to the funding of Cleve Kelso and his billionaire friends. Hidden in an underground facility in the desert, the Skeleton Key can only be unlocked when all five Key Cars are in the proper formation. When Shashi is successful in obtaining the Skeleton Key, the Spy Racers must work together to disarm him and destroy the device.

SEMITRUCKS

While the Spy Racers encounter a number of semitrucks throughout their missions, none is more important than the Yoka Spirit Water truck. It served as the centerpiece of the crew's first undercover heist, and in this truck, their success in stopping Scadan from reaching the border allowed Tony and his team to establish a relationship with SH1FT3R, which helped them bring down the criminal organization from the inside. While Frostee is glad they accomplished the mission, he's even more pumped he found the Yoka Head, which will become his spy command center. And to top it off . . . they've got a truckload of free Yoka. Just another perk of being a Spy Racer!

MOTORCYCLES

While having a souped-up spy car is amazing, sometimes a motorcycle is what's needed to get the job done. Don't let their size fool you, either; these motorcycles have significant advantages, as their riders have more stealth and agility.

Shashi goes undetected when he drives his motorcycle to leap off a cliff, over the ocean, and onto a high-tech super yacht during his successful attempt to steal the first Key Car. On the Las Vegas strip, Layla outruns a heat-seeking missile on her bike, giving the Spy Racers enough time to save the world from the powers of the Skeleton Key. But riding a motorcycle is easier said than done, as Tony will soon learn in Rio. Just don't tell Dom that Tony keeps falling off. He's new at this!

HELICOPTER, PLANE & FIGHTER JETS

HELICOPTER:

This military vehicle transports Cleve Kelso's Key Car to a secure compound for safekeeping.

PLANE:

Ms. Nowhere uses this to track down the Spy Racers after they hijack the spy plane and escape the military compound with Cleve Kelso's Key Car.

FIGHTER JETS:

General Dudley orders his pilots to take down the spy plane after Tony's crew steals the final Key Car. These fighter jets are considered to be faster, sleeker, and more agile than an ordinary aircraft. But the real question is, are they a match for the Spy Racers?

JET SKIS

After successfully destroying the Skeleton Key and saving the world from SH1FT3R, Tony and the crew race Jet Skis for fun while on a much-needed vacation in the Caribbean. Looks like the Spy Racers adhere to the motto "Work hard. Play hard."

YACHT

Shashi steals the first Key Car off the high-tech super yacht owned by one of Cleve Kelso's billionaire friends, despite it having a sophisticated security system and a team of armed guards . . . plus being in the middle of the ocean and all.

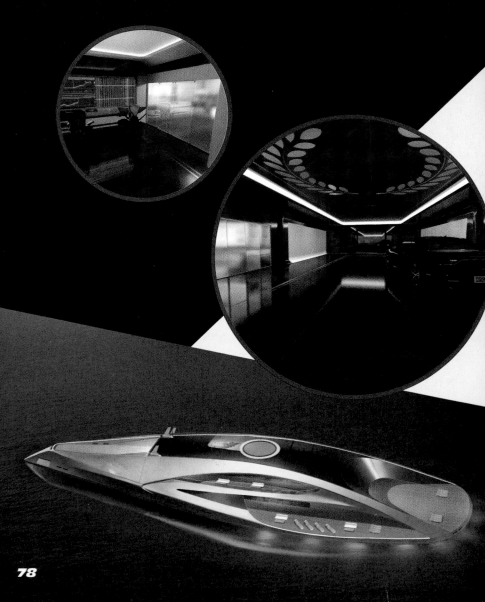

SPEEDBOAT

In one of his most dazzling heists, Shashi successfully infiltrates a high-tech yacht in the middle of the ocean and steals the first Key Car. With nothing but the open water around him, it looks like this thief has no way to escape. Luckily for Shashi, he came prepared.

With the Key Car in gear, Shashi drives off the yacht and lands on an incoming speedboat driven by Layla. But this isn't any ordinary vessel. This one has special netting that is able to grab on to the wheels of the car (or any vehicle, for that matter) and bring it to a quick stop, like a plane landing on an aircraft carrier. It's the perfect boat for the perfect crime.

NEXT MISSION: RIO

The Spy Racers are heading to Brazil for their first international investigation. No matter what happens, they'll always have each other's backs. After all, friends are the best gear a Spy Racer could have.